A SPECIAL THANK YOU
• JUNIOR DISCOVERS INTEGRITY•

BY DAVE RAMSEY
ILLUSTRATED BY MARSHALL RAMSEY

COLLECT ALL SEVEN ADVENTURES AT DAVERAMSEY.COM!

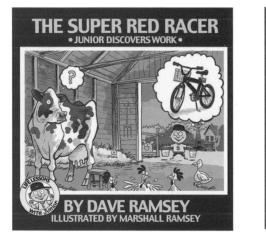

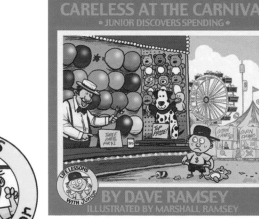

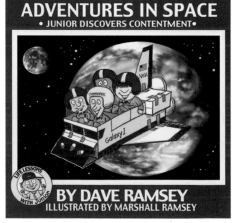

More fun than a barrel of money!

Dedication

To my parents, Tom and Millie—You taught me to work for what
I want and never take what isn't mine. I remember
when I was 4 years old and I took a candy bar from a grocery store.
You made me return it to the store manager. I was embarrassed, but I learned the lesson.
Thank you, Mom and Dad, for teaching me genuine integrity.

Dave

www.daveramsey.com

The children's group of Lampo Press

A Special Thank You: Junior Discovers Integrity
Copyright © 2005 by Lampo Group, Inc.

Requests for information should be addressed to:
Lampo Press: 1749 Mallory Lane Suite #100 Brentwood, Tennessee 37027

ISBN 0-9769630-0-0

First Edition

Written by: Dave Ramsey
Editors: Michele Christy, Amber Kever, Darrin Dickey, Debbie LoCurto
Cover Design and Art Direction: Marshall Ramsey

Printed and bound in China.

For more information on Dave Ramsey, go to: www.daveramsey.com or call (888) 227-3223
For more information on Marshall Ramsey, go to: www.clarionledger.com/ramsey

The school bell rang and everyone ran outside.

"It's Friday!" yelled Junior.

"We get to go to Ida's Ice Palace for Intergalactic Brain Chillers!" yelled Michele.

"I'll race you there," said Billy.

Junior, Billy, Michele and Amber raced down the sidewalk to the store.

"I'm so thirsty!" said Billy, while they waited in line.

"Me, too," said Amber. "I'm getting Rippin' Red Raspberry this time!"

"I want Galaxy Grape!" said Michele.

After they got their Brain Chillers, they sat on a bench outside the store.

Junior stood up. He saw something shiny in the grass. He ran and picked it up. "Look what I found!!!" exclaimed Junior. It was a silver money clip with a ten dollar bill in it. Billy, Amber, and Michele all ran to see.

"Maybe there's MORE!" said Michele. She started looking around and found a twenty dollar bill in the grass! "Oh my goodness, look what I found!" she squealed.

Billy and Amber started searching. They found money, too…a lot of it! The four friends gathered up all of the money, stuffed it in their pockets, and decided to go to their tree house to figure out what to do with it.

They ran as fast as they could to the BIG tree in Junior's yard and climbed the ladder all the way to the top. Once they were all in the tree house, they dumped their money in the middle of the floor.

"What are we going to do with all this money?" asked Junior.

"I think we should count it first to see how much there is," said Billy.

"Good idea," said Michele, as she sorted out the money. She stacked up the one dollar bills and handed them to Junior. She handed Billy all the five dollar bills. Amber started counting the ten dollar bills and Michele counted all of the twenty dollar bills.

"How much do you have, Junior?" asked Billy.

"Ten dollars," replied Junior.

"I have forty dollars," said Billy.

"I have seventy!" exclaimed Amber.

"And I have one hundred!" said Michele.

"That adds up to two hundred and twenty dollars!" said Billy.

Everyone stared in amazement. No one had ever seen that much money before!

"I just got an 'A' on my math test, so I'll split up the money," said Billy. "There," he said, "we each get fifty-five dollars."

"Well, I know what I'll buy with MY money," said Junior. "I'm getting a new skateboard!"

"I'm getting the new Dollar Bill Saves the Day video game," said Billy.

"Well, I'm getting the new Princess Emily doll and her Prince Wesley!" said Michele.

"And I'm going to buy a new tea set and roller blades!" said Amber.

"It's getting late," said Billy. "Let's leave the money here in our secret hiding place for tonight and meet again tomorrow morning. That way we'll have the whole night to think of all the stuff we can buy!"

They all agreed they could use more time to think. So, Junior picked up the money. Billy stood watch at one window. Amber took her place at the other window. Michele lifted the Dollar Bill poster and turned the secret switch. The switch pulled a shoestring that was attached to some dominoes. The dominoes fell over and hit a ball, which traveled through a series of loops and tunnels. Then, the ball smacked into a lever that opened the secret box, where only the most TOP SECRET things were kept. Junior put the pile of money in the box and closed the lid.

That night at dinner Mom asked, "Junior, how was your day?"

"Great!" he answered. "Guess what? I went to Ida's Ice Palace with Billy, Michele and Amber. We found some money on the ground!"

"Wow," replied Mom.

"What are you going to do with it?" asked Dad.

"I don't know. I could use a new skateboard," said Junior.

"Hmmm, did you think about who might have lost that money?" asked Mom. "I know if I lost some money, I'd be very happy if someone returned it to me. I know you'll do the right thing."

That night in his bed, Junior couldn't stop thinking about what Mom meant by doing 'the right thing.' He tossed and turned all night.

The next morning, the four friends met in the tree house.

"Let's count it again, just to make sure!" said Michele.

They took their positions. Billy stood watch at one window. Amber took her place at the other window. Michele turned the secret switch. Junior opened the TOP SECRET box.

"Got it!" said Junior, as he took out the money.

Billy recounted the money. Every dollar was there—two hundred and twenty dollars. He sorted out the money, "one for you, and one for you, and one for you, one for me…" They each stuffed their money in their pockets and climbed down the ladder. Then, they rode their bikes to Neal's Neat-O Toys—their favorite store!

At Neal's Neat-O Toys, they ran through the aisles to grab their new toys. Junior and Billy picked out the coolest skateboard. They were headed for the video game aisle when they ran into Amber and Michele. The girls were trying to decide which dolls to buy.

Suddenly, Junior heard his mom's voice in his head, "If I lost some money, I'd be very happy if someone returned it to me." He felt sick to his stomach. At first, he thought it might have been that humongous chocolate Zappo bar he ate earlier. Nope, that wasn't it. Again, he remembered his mom saying, "I know you'll do the RIGHT THING!" He knew that the money they found belonged to someone else.

"Wait!" he said. "I think we need to do SOMETHING ELSE with the money."

"Oh! I know! We could put our money together and buy something REALLY cool like a stereo for the tree house!" said Amber.

"No, I mean…well…this isn't really OUR money. We just found it, right?" asked Junior. "Well, if YOU lost YOUR money, wouldn't you want someone to return it to YOU?"

SALE!
$199.99

CD-R

They all just stared at him for a minute.

"I think Junior's right," said Michele. "I lost my lunch money last week and Jennifer found it and gave it back to me. I was really thankful."

"Yeah, I guess we should give it back. But, who do we give it to? We don't know who lost it," said Billy.

Just then, Barry, the policeman, walked by and saw the children in a serious discussion.

"Good afternoon, children," said Policeman Barry. "Looks like you are buying quite a few toys today. What's the occasion?"

Junior spoke up, "Well, sir, we found this money on the ground yesterday and we wanted to buy toys, but we realized that it isn't our money. We want to give it back, but we don't know who to give it to."

"Well, kids, I think you're doing the RIGHT THING by returning the money," said Policeman Barry. "Why don't you have your mom take you down to the police station later this afternoon and I'll meet you there. We can put the money in our Lost and Found box and wait for someone to claim it. If no one claims it, then it's yours to keep. Fair enough?"

They all thought that was a good idea. They put their toys back on the shelves and headed for Junior's house. After lunch, Junior's mom took them to the police station. They met Policeman Barry and put the money in the Lost and Found box.

The next day, Mom got a call from Policeman Barry. "Junior, Policeman Barry called to tell us that Mr. Webb claimed the money you kids found. Apparently, he lost it while he was running some errands. He was very happy to get it back!"

"You sure did the RIGHT THING. I knew you would," said Dad, as he patted Junior on the head.

Later that day, Old Man Webb called.

"Junior, this phone call is for you," said Mom.

"Hello?" said Junior.

"Hello, this is Mr. Webb. Policeman Barry told me that you found my money. Thank you for returning it to me. Ask your parents if they'll walk you and your friends to my house this afternoon."

"I'll ask them. See you later," replied Junior.

Junior called Billy, Amber and Michele. They came to Junior's house right away.

"I wonder what Old Man Webb wants?" asked Billy.

"I don't know," said Junior.

About that time Junior's dad yelled, "Let's go!"

They all walked down the street to Old Man Webb's house a few blocks away.

Junior reached up and rang the doorbell. After a few moments Old Man Webb opened the door and invited them all in.

"Hello, everyone," said Old Man Webb, as he began shaking their hands. "Thank you for coming to my house."

"I am very proud of you all," he said. "It was the right thing to do, returning that money. A lot of children would have kept it for themselves. You children have INTEGRITY!"

They all stared at each other with empty expressions.

"Do you know what integrity is?" he asked. Without waiting for an answer, he explained, "It's doing the RIGHT THING, even when no one is looking…and not expecting anything in return. That's INTEGRITY. And you have it, children."

Junior and his friends smiled at each other.

"I like having IN-TEG-RI-TY," said Junior.

"It's a very good thing to have," said Old Man Webb. "I want to give you a very SPECIAL THANK YOU for having INTEGRITY and returning my money. You probably weren't expecting anything, but I think you'll like this." Old Man Webb walked to his door and said, "Follow me." He led the whole group down the sidewalk.

"Where are we going?" whispered Michele.

"I don't know," said Amber. "But, he said we would like it!"

After a few blocks, they turned a corner and arrived at Neal's Neat-O Toys. Old Man Webb got out his key and began unlocking the door.

"Do you work here?" asked Amber.

"Sometimes...but I also OWN the toy store," answered Old Man Webb with a twinkle in his eye.

"I want you children to pick out one toy as a SPECIAL THANK YOU for having integrity," he said.

"WOW!" they all exclaimed.

Junior smiled ear to ear as he ran down the aisle to get his skateboard. He turned around and said, "Thank you for the gift, Mr. Webb!"

SALE!